STACY M. JONES

The 1922 Club Murder

A Mystery Novella

First published by Stacy M. Jones 2019

First edition

This book was professionally typeset on Reedsy.
Find out more at reedsy.com

For Little Rock friends who welcomed me into your city & the unbelievable support you've given on this writing journey.

Contents

Acknowledgement

The 1922 Club Murder would not have been created without a wonderful creative team working with me. A special thanks to Sharon Aponte with Chick & a Mouse Graphic Design for the great cover, and Dj Hendrickson for her invaluable editing and suggestions. To all my readers and those who continue to support me – thank you.

CHAPTER 1

My editor at the Little Rock Record called the 1922 Club a hotbed of illegal activity. The club, with its mansard style design, was originally constructed as a home for a wealthy Arkansas politician. Built in 1870, it graces a corner slice of Cantrell Road before the road turns into La Harpe Boulevard in downtown Little Rock. The house's backyard backs right up to the Arkansas River, which made it the perfect spot for Little Rock's most notorious speakeasy during Prohibition. Alcohol came right off a boat and into the house under the cover of night. That's how the club garnered its current name.

In 1922, bootleggers bought the grand home and took up residence. They used parts of the house as living quarters while turning the rest into a speakeasy. The second floor became a private bar that was accessed from the original servants' back staircase. If a visitor didn't know the secret password, entrance from the back porch up the stairs was denied. The bar itself was ornately designed, and after a refurbish, is still the bar of the 1922 Club today.

The house is everything people say it is. It's grand, somewhat eerie and always seems to keep its notorious reputation. The 1922 Club is a social club for politicians, lawyers and business leaders, but its exclusivity and high membership price tag keep the locals talking about what really goes on behind those walls.

I had only been in the place once. The newspaper had a reception in the dining room, and we were provided a tour. The club has a center hall that runs the length of the building from the large front foyer to the back. The main dining rooms take up two large rooms on the left, and on the right is a library room and an informal sitting room, which also has a side door that leads to a covered walkway, connecting to the driveway and back parking area. Years ago, the back of the home was converted into a large commercial kitchen. The second floor, which is accessed by the grand staircase in the front of the home off the foyer and the back staircase, has a few offices. It is mostly the bar area with oversized leather chairs and sofas and billiards tables. The third floor has private meeting spaces that can be rented. Nearly all of the rooms have been renovated back to their formal glory when the home had first been constructed.

I was currently standing with a sea of other reporters on the sidewalk at the base of the club's driveway waiting for an official statement from the Little Rock Police Department. There had been a murder. Earlier this morning when the club's director came to work, she found the chef's body in the main dining room. All we knew was that he was dead from an apparent stab wound, or at least that was the gossip among the reporters.

Chef Andre Mouton had been the club's chef for the last four years. He also owned and managed several restaurants in Little Rock. Locally, he was fairly famous. He had been featured in *Bon Appétit, Southern Living Magazine,* and others, bringing a real sense of foodie culture to the city. Now he was dead.

As soon as I walked into the office this morning, my editor, Dan Barnes, yelled for me. The entire news floor heard, "Riley

Sullivan, don't even take off your coat. Get your ass to the 1922 Club. Chef has been murdered." After a collective gasp was heard around the newsroom, I made a beeline to the scene.

That was more than two hours ago, and I still didn't have any other details than that. Dan had already called me twice. He was not pleased to hear I still didn't have a story. He knew there was nothing more I could do, but he was a grouch. I liked him, probably more than any other reporter at the paper, but I wasn't a native southerner. Until a year ago, I lived in upstate New York where I grew up and still had family, including my mother, sister and an ex-husband. Dan's straightforward, no nonsense personality suited me fine. When he was yelling at me, it was a bit like being back home. I took it in stride. Mostly, I thought he just needed a date. He was divorced, no kids, and married to the paper.

Most of the reporters standing near me were complaining about the cold. It wasn't bad, but then again, I was used to blizzards in upstate. Anything above freezing, I was fine. The wind made me pull my jacket around me a bit tighter and I wished I had brought gloves.

From my vantage point, I could see the medical examiner's staff wheel a black body bag on a stretcher out of the side entrance of the home and into the back of the van. Following right behind them were several Little Rock Police Department detectives including my boyfriend, Lucas "Luke" Morgan, and his long-time friend Cooper Deagnan. They had been friends since college, both thirty-four and standing about six foot. They made detective the same year. That's where the comparisons stopped.

Luke was black, bald by choice and was as straight-laced as they came. He was proving himself to be a fantastic detective.

3

He worked well in the structure of the department. On the other hand, Cooper, blond and green-eyed, was not cut out for police work. He was a great detective but all the rules, regulations and paperwork frequently hung him up. At least once an investigation, he told Luke he was going to quit and just become a private investigator. While Luke talked him out of it each time, I thought it was a great plan.

I watched the two of them speak to the crime scene investigators and then start to make their way down the driveway with Captain Kurt Meadows. I had never met him, but Luke told me often how much he liked Captain Meadows. He frequently said how smart he was and how well he ran the detective's bureau. With retirement looming, Luke wasn't sure how long he'd be around.

Captain Meadows' booming voice quieted the group of reporters. Cameras turned on, photographers snapped photos and reporters like me turned on their digital recorders to capture the statement. He said, "At approximately eight-twenty-five this morning, Shana Ellis, director of the 1922 Club, found Chef Andre Mouton dead on the floor of the dining room. It looks like he had been stabbed several times. There are no immediate suspects at this time. We ask the public with any information to contact the department and speak to Det. Lucas Morgan, who will lead this investigation. That's all we have at this time."

Reporters lobbed a series of questions, trying to gain more information, but Captain Meadows just reiterated the details from the statement with a promise of more information when it became available. I had the basics for a story. I caught Luke's eye before I left. I smiled, and he nodded his head at me. I figured he'd text me later to catch up.

CHAPTER 2

"What do you think, Luke?" Captain Meadows inquired.

Luke, Cooper, and Captain Meadows were standing inside the dining room of the 1922 Club. The crime scene investigators had finished their work, the reporters from the press conference had left, and the three of them were back inside the building to talk over the crime. They stood around the dining room near the spot were Chef Mouton had been found face down.

Luke looked around. It was a large room, taking up what would have probably been the dining and formal living room of the original house. The high ceilings, hardwoods, and dark wood wainscoting along with the ornate fireplace gave the dining space a comfortable, inviting feel. Most of the tables had linens and were set for lunch.

Nothing seemed out of place other than a large amount of blood pooled in one area of the floor where Chef's body was found and one table they assumed was knocked over when he fell. Luke walked to the back of the room to the double doors that lead into the commercial kitchen. He stepped in and back out again.

He looked at his Captain and explained, "I think it's someone who knew Chef and caught him by surprise. There's no sign of struggle. Chef isn't just going to let someone stab him, and from what we could see, most of the wounds are to his back so maybe they snuck up on him. We don't know what kind of knife yet, but there's certainly an abundance of knives right in the kitchen. We'll need to talk to the kitchen staff to see if any are missing."

"Chef was similar to Luke and me in size. I don't know how strong he was but seemed like it didn't take much to overpower him," Cooper commented.

"What's he, about six foot and a hundred and ninety pounds give or take?" Captain Meadows wondered.

"Yeah, that's about what he was. Cooper's right. It wouldn't take much, especially if they came up and stabbed him from behind," Luke added.

"Let's try something," Luke suggested and moved Cooper close to where Chef's body was found, avoiding the blood still pooled on the floor. "Stand there, Coop, and look out into the dining room. I want to see if you can hear me walking up behind you."

Luke walked back to the kitchen and approached Cooper from the back. Luke was quiet, taking soft, careful steps. He couldn't be sure exactly where the killer came from, but given where Chef was found, they had a decent idea.

Luke got within a few steps of Cooper and the floor creaked. The sound was loud and obvious against the silent backdrop of the rest of the house. Luke stepped to the side and the same thing happened.

Cooper turned, "It was loud enough that if it was me, I would have turned to see who was there. I'd think we'd see more signs of a struggle."

Luke agreed. "That's what I was thinking. Maybe it was someone he knew or someone he was expecting. Someone in the room with him. There's no trail of blood so it all happened here, but someone obviously got the drop on him."

"Maybe," Captain Meadows said matter-of-factly. He looked to Luke, "Where is the woman that found him?"

"She's outside speaking to one of the uniformed guys. She's giving a brief statement. I told her I'd formally interview her at the station. She found him, but she doesn't strike me as someone who could have killed him. She was pretty distraught on the call to 911. As a precaution, I've kept her out of the scene."

"Let's bring her back in," Captain Meadows suggested. He walked to the side door that led to the driveway. A few minutes later he walked in with Shana Ellis. She had an average build, stood about five-six and had long brown hair. She was pretty but understated.

Luke and Cooper introduced themselves again. Luke asked, "Could you walk us through what happened this morning?"

Shana nodded. "It started like any other morning. I came in a little before eight-thirty when I usually arrive. I pulled my car around back and came through the side entrance. The back entrance goes directly upstairs and into the kitchen on the first floor so I never use that. I always come in the side, directly into the reception area or sitting room as most people call it. As I moved into the hall, I saw Chef face down on the floor in the dining room. I ran over to him but stopped when I saw blood. I tried to check for his pulse, but I couldn't find it. I got scared and ran out and called 911."

"Did you touch anything else?" Luke asked. He noted the blood on the right sleeve of her shirt, probably from where she reached to check his pulse.

Shana shook her head no. She started to cry, "I can't believe this happened."

Cooper asked, "Do you know of anyone that might have wanted to hurt Chef or any issues at work?"

Shana took a tissue from her purse and wiped her eyes. "I heard him arguing a few weeks ago with someone on the phone, but I don't know who. His voice was raised and he sounded upset. I didn't hear what he was saying. He wasn't always the easiest person to work with. The sous-chef, Miles Carter, had been here longer than Chef. He's been angry for a long time that he was passed over for the executive chef position. I know there was tension but nothing to the level of this."

Captain Meadows excused himself to head back to the station. Luke and Cooper walked Shana through the club to see if anything seemed out of place or was missing. She didn't see anything, but she confirmed to Luke he'd need to ask kitchen staff about the knives. She had no idea.

When they were back in the dining room, Shana looked down at the blood and then back to Luke. "Obviously I need to get a cleaning crew in here, but do we need to stay closed or can we reopen? I just need to put out notice either way."

"Keep it closed for the next few days. Tell the staff they have to stay out. I'll have some uniformed cops here keeping an eye on the place. We might need access. We'll let you know as soon as you can reopen."

Shana sighed. "How long do you think? Our members won't be happy."

"Just a few days at most. Do you really think people will want to be relaxing and eating in here after a murder?"

"You don't know our members. This will only make this place

8

more appealing," Shana said, rolling her eyes with a regretful nod of her head.

CHAPTER 3

"What have you got for me, kid?" Dan called out as I made my way back into the newsroom. The newspaper's office was located on Capitol Avenue not too far from the 1922 Club. I had stopped at Doe's Eat Place, a local favorite, on my way back. I dropped my coat on my desk and carried the bag with my cheeseburger and fries along with my notepad and pen into Dan's office. I bumped the door closed with my hip.

Dan looked up from his desk, saw the bag of greasy food and shook his head disapprovingly. "Thought you were on a diet?"

"Thought you had enough sense not to ask a woman a stupid question," I said sarcastically. "I'm hungry and stressed so let it go. And stop calling me kid, I'm three years younger than you."

Dan laughed. "I like you, Yankee. Sit, eat but tell me what you know."

I plopped all my stuff down on Dan's side table and took a seat. I unwrapped my cheeseburger and took a huge satisfying bite. Dan was right. I should have been on a diet. I said I was, but today wasn't the day. My curves would have to wait. I savored another bite like it would be my last. Dan was looking at me expectantly. He could wait, too. When I swallowed, I said, "Chef's dead. Looks like stab wounds. He was found by Shana

Ellis, the director of the club. From what it seems, he hadn't been dead long and the cops have no leads."

"How do you know they have no leads?" Dan looked at me with his bushy dark eyebrows raised.

"The cops said as much. They made no arrest, didn't seem to be in a hurry to run off anywhere and the only witness we know of, who found the body, was not in custody. No leads."

Dan laughed because he knew I was right. He underestimated me, but then again, he underestimated all his reporters. "I know you didn't just go to Doe's for the burger so what did you hear?"

It was my turn to laugh. I took another bite of my burger and grabbed a few fries. "It seems Chef has had a few failed restaurants. One in New Orleans, another in Memphis. He owed some people money. I also heard he was having an affair with a married woman." I checked my notebook. "Rhonda McCreery. Seems Rhonda has a husband."

"You have the husband's name?"

"Marcus McCreery. Someone said he's a boxer. Any idea?"

Dan nodded yes. "He's definitely a boxer. He's retired from fighting though. He won his last match a few years back. But he owns a local boxing gym. He's a big guy. I could see him doing some damage if he caught his wife cheating."

"Definitely seems like enough leads to start digging," I said and finished the last of my food. "Maybe I'll pay Marcus a visit. I can always pretend I'm looking to workout."

"Is that one of those things I'm not supposed to comment on?" Dan looked at me, a crooked smile on his face.

"You're learning," I teased. "Seriously, though, maybe I can go chat him up and see if he has an alibi."

"You're just going to waltz into the gym and investigate him?" Dan asked with a hint of skepticism in his voice.

"He's not going to know I'm investigating him, just make small talk."

"I see," Dan said. He started to gather up some papers, which was usually a sign he was done talking to whoever was in his office, but he continued, "What's your boyfriend have to say about the case?"

"Dan," I said with an exaggerated sigh, "you know I don't take advantage like that."

Dan laid the paper down on his desk. He looked me in the eyes, barely containing a laugh. "You're so full of it. We both know as soon as you get the chance, you're going to grill him for info, even if it's off the record. It's what you're best at. Great for work, but I'd sure the hell hate dating you."

"Don't worry, you won't ever have to experience dating me. We'd kill each other."

Dan just shook his head at me and laughed. I gathered up my things and headed for the door. Right as I walked out, he called, "If you get in trouble with the boxer, give me a shout."

CHAPTER 4

I navigated out of downtown Little Rock and up the Cantrell hill. I was heading back towards my house located in the Heights neighborhood of Little Rock. I lived on N. Tyler Street in a 1925 Craftsman that I renovated shortly after I moved to the city and ended a very tumultuous relationship. I passed by my street and headed farther out into West Little Rock where the boxing gym was located. It was a half mile on the right past Pleasant Ridge Town Center. The gym was in a warehouse that looked industrial. I parked, appraised myself in my mirror and tried to tame my long auburn hair. Once pin straight, now that I was two years into my thirties, my hair had developed a natural wave I couldn't seem to do much with so I didn't. It did its own thing.

As soon as I opened the door to the gym, the smell knocked me back. It was raw sweat, masculine and overpowering. I scanned around the room and didn't see Marcus. I had pulled up a photo from the internet so I had a vague idea of what he looked like, but all the men here seemed to fit the same meaty mold.

From my left a man was approaching. He could be Marcus, but I wasn't sure. He looked me up and down and found me wanting. His look of disgust told me I didn't belong.

He frowned at me and asked, "Can I help you?"

"I thought about taking some boxing classes, and I heard this was the place to come."

"You box?" he asked skeptically, attempting poorly to hide his laughter.

"I've been known to handle myself. My father was a boxer when he was in his twenties." That was technically true. Patrick Sullivan was a boxer in his youth, but he and my mother Karen divorced early on, and I barely knew the man, other than by reputation as an Irish mobster living in Ireland. I could handle my own though. At five-seven, I was curvy but not fat. I was thick-hipped and far from flat-chested. I was strong, too.

He circled around me and motioned me to follow him. He brought me to a mat in the far back of the room. I took off my coat and dropped my bag. I wasn't dressed for boxing but had worn a simple long-sleeve tee-shirt and pants so I was good enough. He handed me boxing gloves. I rolled up my sleeves before I put them on.

"We'll see how good you are," he said with a smirk.

"You have a name? I'm Riley."

"Jimmy. I'm one of the trainers here. Hands up. Let's go."

He had a few inches and probably thirty pounds of muscle on me. I was fairly certain he could kick my ass. He started to throw a few jabs that I was able to deflect. He was going easy on me, but I could tell he was a bit surprised I had any moves. I got a bit gutsier and took a few jabs of my own. He deflected them but said, "You don't hit like a girl, but you're still soft. Come on, Snickers, put your full weight behind it."

I nearly laughed at the name. I didn't even like the candy, and I liked the man taking jabs at me even less. I swung harder and he did as well, neither of us connecting. We bobbed and weaved around the mat. We were stopped by a deep male voice off to the left. He yelled, "Jimmy, what the hell are you thinking? Stop that right now." Jimmy turned just as I had thrown a punch. It connected with his jaw. It took both of us by surprise. He turned back to me quickly with fire in his eyes. He didn't get to take a swing though because the other man yelled at him to stop.

"I'll get you back for that one," Jimmy snarled and sulked off.

I took my gloves off and caught my breath. The man, dressed in running pants and a Razorback tee-shirt, his muscles clearly outlined and straining the fabric, put his hand out to me. "I'm Marcus McCreery, owner here. Sorry about Jimmy. We don't have many women that come in. The ones we do are already in fighting shape. You've got a great right hook though. What can I do for you?"

"I was looking to start exercising again and heard boxing was a good way to go."

Marcus shook his head no. "We aren't the place for you. We're here for serious boxers. You should try the kickboxing club down the road." He started to walk off.

I wasn't giving up that easily. "Do you know Chef Mouton with the 1922 Club? He's the one that recommended I come see you."

He turned on me and closed the distance in a few steps. I could tell I rattled him. He bore down on me. "Who are you really?"

I put my hands up in surrender. "I don't understand why you're so upset. He said this gym was a great place to train so I'm here. If you're not interested in assisting me, I can go elsewhere." I turned to leave, but he grabbed me by the shoulder.

He said angrily, "You're not going anywhere until I get some answers."

Marcus was hurting me, his hand gripping my shoulder and squeezing too tightly. I was sure he'd leave a bruise. Before I could say anything, I heard a familiar voice come from behind me.

"I think you should let the woman go. It looks like she's trying to leave," Luke said sternly, holding up his badge. Luke and Cooper were standing at the front door of the gym. Neither of them looked happy to see me. Even though I knew Luke and I would get into it later, I was happy to see him. More than that, Marcus' reaction told me he had something to hide when it came to Chef Mouton. His reaction was too over the top.

I turned to Marcus and then back to Luke. "I was just leaving. I can see myself out."

I grabbed my bag and coat and headed for the door. Marcus glared at me the entire time. Luke followed me. As I opened the door to leave, he said barely above a whisper, "You shouldn't be interfering in my investigation. We'll talk about this tonight."

This wouldn't be the first and certainly not the last time we'd have this debate.

CHAPTER 5

L uke watched Riley walk to her car. It wasn't the first time she had gotten a jump on him in an investigation. Her being at the gym sealed the deal for Luke that the tip they had about Chef's affair was a solid one. Riley didn't run down rabbit holes chasing every lead. Luke was angry that she was here, but more than anything, he was glad he showed up when he did. When Luke was sure Riley was safe in her car, he turned to Marcus and said evenly, "Let's continue that conversation you two were having."

"What do you mean?" Marcus asked. He looked down to his feet and didn't meet Luke's gaze.

"Chef Mouton was found dead this morning. We believe you know him."

Marcus looked a little bit shocked. "A lot of people know him."

"Let's not play games," Luke chided. "We can talk out here or maybe you have a private office to have this discussion."

Marcus hitched his jaw to the right. Both Cooper and Luke followed him across the gym and up a flight of stairs. Once they were in an office and seated at a round table positioned in the middle of the room, Cooper asked, "How do you know Chef Mouton?"

"I don't know him, really," Marcus said. He took a deep breath and explained. "He was having an affair with my wife, Rhonda. I just found out about it a couple weeks ago."

"How'd you find out?" Luke asked.

"My wife isn't the sharpest, if you know what I mean. I followed her one night to his house. I followed her another time to make sure."

"Did you confront them?"

Marcus shook his head no. "I wanted to but figured it would end eventually."

Luke sat back in the chair and appraised the man in front of him. He was a big man, taller than Luke. His arms were strong solid muscle, bigger than most men Luke had encountered. He had a mean looking mug on him. You could tell his face had taken a beating from his boxing days. Nothing about the man told Luke he'd sit by while some guy was giving it to his wife.

Luke exchanged a look with Cooper. He leaned forward resting his arms on the table, looking Marcus in the eyes. "We're going to give you a chance to tell us the truth because I don't believe that for a second. I'll ask a different question. When did you confront Chef and what happened when you did?"

Marcus started to protest. For a second, Luke wondered if he'd refuse to speak to them at all. But Marcus snapped, "The second night I followed Rhonda. I went to the door, knocked and shoved my way in his house when he answered. I punched him, roughed him up a bit, but he was alive when I left. I pulled Rhonda out of there, and we've been trying to work things out ever since."

Cooper inquired, "When was that?"

"A few weeks back. I don't know the date."

"Where were you last night into early this morning?" Luke

18

asked. He believed that Marcus had roughed up Chef, but Luke wasn't positive that's all he did.

"I was home last night with Rhonda. I came into the gym about five this morning. You can check with my staff. I met two of the trainers to let them in. We sparred a few rounds, and I've been in my office since then."

"We'll need to talk to those trainers," Cooper said.

Marcus made a quick phone call. A few minutes later both trainers, Jimmy and Chris, confirmed that Marcus had met them right at five that morning and had been at the gym for the rest of the day.

Marcus then offered to call Rhonda, but Cooper and Luke declined. They said they'd speak with her directly. Luke and Cooper shared a knowing look. Cooper excused himself from the meeting and went to make a call outside. He was calling Rhonda before Marcus had a chance to fill her in on the conversation. They had her number and planned to speak with her but wanted to see what Marcus would say first.

Luke continued on. "You have any idea why someone else would want to kill Chef?"

"Don't know and don't care. I didn't kill him, but I'm not sorry he's dead." Marcus folded his thick arms over his chest. "We about done?"

"Did you see the news this morning announcing that Chef was dead?"

"No."

"You aren't curious then how he died or where he was found?"

"Not really. Just one more dead scumbag. Why would I care how he went out?"

"You clearly hated the man. I thought it would have at least sparked your curiosity." Luke wasn't sure where he was going

19

with this. He just wanted to see the man's reactions.

Marcus shrugged, clearly bored with the conversation. "Fine. Where was he found? How was he killed?"

"Chef was found in the dining room of the 1922 Club. He had several stab wounds. Looked pretty personal, like the person who killed him was pretty angry."

"See that's where I got you detective. That's not how I would have killed him." Marcus held up both hands, making two fists. "Why would I stab him when I could just beat him to death?"

Luke thought that was probably the most honest thing the guy said. Luke got up to leave and as he walked out the door, he said, "We'll be in touch."

CHAPTER 6

I ran down a few more leads that didn't amount to much. I stopped at the Starbucks on Kavanaugh to bang out four hundred words for the digital edition of the paper and for the morning print news. I told Dan it was submitted. He wasn't pleased I didn't get more, but he trusted that if I had, I would have told him. I wondered if Luke had gotten anywhere with Marcus. I thought I was on the brink of getting some information when Luke interrupted. Hopefully, he got the info I didn't.

Before leaving Starbucks, I called my friend Emma. She and her husband Joe lived next door to me. They had the sweetest baby girl. Sophie was just four months old. Both Joe and Emma looked exhausted every time I saw them. When Emma answered, I told her I was picking them up dinner and wanted to see if they had any special requests. She didn't but professed her undying gratitude. Besides Luke and Cooper, Emma and Joe were the best friends I had in Little Rock.

I stopped at Heights Taco & Tamale, just a few steps from Starbucks, and then made my way over the short couple blocks to our houses on N. Tyler Street. Emma met me at her door with Sophie on her hip. Emma still had a bit of baby weight that just fleshed out her normally thin frame. Her naturally dark hair was a bit longer than her typical bob, but I liked it longer. She always had a smile for me. Sophie was my goddaughter. I pinched her sweet little cheeks and gave Emma a hug before stepping inside.

"They find any more on Chef Mouton today?" Emma asked as I dropped the bag of food on her kitchen counter.

"There's a few leads. I heard Chef was having an affair with a married woman so I went to run down that lead, but Luke and Cooper showed up at the same time," I explained, rolling my eyes. Emma was my best friend in the world. I could share all of my secrets with her, even about work.

Emma laughed. "He must be thrilled you're interfering in his investigation."

"He's so high strung sometimes. I'm a crime reporter. I have leads I have to run down to get my story. If we cross paths, that's not really my problem."

Emma strapped Sophie into her baby seat. Sophie smiled and cooed, making all kinds of sweet baby noises. "When are you letting him move in?"

"Not ready yet."

Emma frowned at me. She thought Luke and I were perfect together, and I couldn't disagree. It didn't mean I was ready to take that big of a leap.

"He's not going to wait forever. If you love him, move forward. You need to get over the past. Luke isn't George," Emma said, leveling a look at me.

"You're right. I just need to take the leap, but I'm finding it harder than I thought it would be. I really don't want to get hurt again."

"No one wants to get hurt, Riley. But it doesn't mean you avoid life. Besides, I'm fairly certain Luke would do anything for you."

I nodded. There wasn't much I could say. Emma was right. George Brewer was an ex-boyfriend. We had met while I was in New York. We dated for a while, and it eventually led to a move to be closer to him, which is what brought me to Little Rock. It was only after I moved that I learned he was engaged to another woman, Maime LaRue. He's since married her. I didn't want it to, but it changed my perception on love.

Emma looked at me. She seemed to be debating telling me something. Finally, she spoke, softly asking, "Speaking of George, have you talked to him lately?"

I hated talking about him. "Yeah, he called me a couple days ago. He wanted to meet for lunch, but I told him no. Why?"

Emma sized me up. She crossed her arms and looked me square in the eyes. "Maime drove by the house again. I saw her the other night and again early this morning."

Emma sat down at the table and pulled me down in the chair next to her. She put her arm on mine and gave me that look she gives. She's really the perfect mom already.

"I know this has been going on for too long," I conceded. It had been. When Maime had found out about me, she and her friends harassed me with calls and emails for weeks and drove by my place. I didn't understand it. When I found out about her, I walked away. She fought to keep him. Seems she's still fighting to keep him, but it's a battle she's in by herself.

"You need to tell Luke so he can put a stop to it," Emma urged. "It's not normal. You've moved on. You're dating someone else, and she's stalking you."

I knew Emma was right, but I also didn't feel like dealing with it. I kept hoping it would just go away on its own. I didn't feel like reliving my stupidity for getting involved with him.

"I will," I assured her. "I'm just going to let Luke get through this case, and I'll tell him. And on that note, I'm heading home. Tell Joe I said hi and enjoy dinner."

CHAPTER 7

I made my way back to my house and grabbed a few things then headed to Luke's house on Walnut Street in Hillcrest. We had exchanged keys a few months back so I let myself in and got comfortable. I started a fire in the fireplace and flipped through some notes I had about the case. I didn't have much. I placed a quick call to Rhonda, the woman Chef was having an affair with, but I got her voicemail. I headed to the kitchen with the intention of heating some leftovers we had for dinner the previous night when I heard Luke's key in the lock. I put the food back in the fridge and headed to the door.

"I came over so you could yell at me," I said sarcastically as Luke and Cooper came through the door.

They exchanged a glance and came in. Luke gave me a quick hug. "I'd like to, but we've had this fight before. You're just doing your job, and I'm doing mine. But you know if you got a lead, you should have called me."

"You ever just going to call us when you're supposed to or is Luke wasting his breath?" Cooper asked sarcastically.

"What do you think?" I asked, standing with my hands on my hips and a smirk on my face.

"That's what I thought." Cooper laughed and patted me on the head. "You're lucky we like you. You don't make this easy on us."

I slapped his hand away. I met Cooper right after I met Luke. He introduced me shortly after we started dating. Cooper and I became fast friends. To me, he wasn't just my boyfriend's friend. He was my friend, too. Cooper treated me like the sister he didn't have.

"We have some leftover lasagna in the fridge if either of you want it. I was just going to heat some up. There's salad and bread, too."

The three of us headed into the kitchen. We bumped around, making plates of food and getting drinks before sitting down at Luke's small kitchen table. "Hear anymore from the medical examiner or crime scene techs?" I asked.

Luke and Cooper both looked at me over their plates. Luke smiled. "You don't give up, do you?"

"Nope. Never."

Luke took a few more bites of food. Then he asked like he always does if it's off the record. I don't know why we have to go through this ritual every single time, but I guess it makes him feel better. I sighed. "Of course it's off the record until you tell me I can run with it. I'd never break that trust."

Luke set his fork down and explained. "Chef had been dead about an hour, maybe less. Shana was lucky she didn't get there any sooner or she might have encountered the killer. We ruled her out already. Solid alibi and no real motive."

"Since you clearly interrupted my stellar interviewing skills with Marcus this morning," I said sarcastically, "what did you get after I was banished?"

Cooper finished his bite of food and washed it down with his sweet tea. "He's clearly angry. Said he roughed up Chef a bit, but he seems to have a solid alibi, too. I called Rhonda and his story checks out. He confronted them and the affair ended. Rhonda doesn't have an alibi, but I don't think she's good for it. Marcus said he left her asleep at home in bed when he left, and Rhonda said she woke up to the news. She seemed quite upset. The affair may have ended, but I don't think the feelings did."

Luke agreed with Cooper and then added, "Marcus also made an odd but probably truthful point before I left. He said he didn't need to stab him, he would have just beat him to death."

I shook my head in disgust. "That's gruesome."

I picked up my plate and headed for the sink. I offered them more food, but both declined. "Did you hear anything about bad business deals and Chef owing people money?"

Luke looked surprised. "No, not yet."

"I got a tip while down at Doe's. I heard he went bankrupt on some restaurants out of state and left his investors in the lurch. I wonder how his restaurants here were doing."

Cooper laughed. "How the hell are you always one step ahead of us?"

I shrugged. "People talk to me. Plus, I'm not a cop so when I ask questions, people are more readily eager to engage me in conversation. Not everyone knows I'm a reporter."

"You have any names or any other details on that?" Luke asked.

"No, I was going to research tomorrow."

"No, you're not. You're going to leave that to us, and if we get anything we want to run with, we will call you," Luke warned. "I mean it, Riley. We are thankful for the tip, but the Captain will be breathing down my neck if we mess up this case."

"I'll do what I can, but I still have a job to do," I said defiantly. I saw Cooper checking his watch. "You need to go?" I asked.

Cooper cleared his throat. "Yeah, I've got company coming

over."

Luke and I waited for more, but he didn't elaborate. Cooper was always single. He could be the hottest bachelor in town if he wanted, but so far, he had avoided entanglements so we were definitely curious. But he was out the door before we could get any information from him.

As soon as Cooper left, Luke got up and pulled me into his arms. Not that we were hiding our relationship, but Luke was cautious about letting anyone from work see how serious it was. Even though Cooper was a friend, I think he still worried about the other detectives making too big of a deal about getting serious with a journalist. It was a cop thing.

Luke kissed me passionately. "Thanks for dinner. You spending the night?"

I looked up into his eyes. "Not tonight. I'm really tired and just want to settle in at home and go to sleep. Tomorrow night?"

His kiss was response enough.

As soon as I was back home, I couldn't help myself. I pulled out my laptop and started researching Chef's businesses. It didn't mean I was going to do anything with the information, but I wasn't just going to sit and do nothing.

CHAPTER 8

L uke met Purvis at the medical examiner's office first thing in the morning. Purvis had called to tell Luke there was evidence he wanted to go over. Luke went there before heading into the station. He came alone because Cooper was running down some leads connected to Chef's restaurants. It was a good tip Riley had given them, and they ran with it. Luke's regular partner Det. Bill Tyler, who was on leave due to knee surgery, had made a couple calls to help them pin down Chef's current investors. Cooper was paying each a visit.

Purvis escorted Luke back into the medical suite where he conducted the autopsies. Once inside, Purvis walked up to a metal table that held Chef's body and pulled the sheet back. "The stab wounds to his back were fairly obvious given the way he had fallen, and with the amount of blood he lost, it was hard to tell much else on the scene."

Purvis pointed to a stab wound to Chef's abdomen. "We didn't see this at the scene, but it looks like this is where he was stabbed first. It's a fairly straight stab wound, like he walked right into it. I'm not seeing an angle on the entry. The wounds on the back I think were made as he was falling or maybe already on the ground."

Luke assessed the knife wound and could see what Purvis was talking about. It did look like Chef walked right into the blade. "Did you confirm what kind of knife?"

"Looks like a typical eight-inch all-purpose chef's knife. Do you know yet if anything is missing from the kitchen?"

"No, I've got a walkthrough with the sous-chef later today. That's the first thing I'm checking other than his alibi. We wanted to interview him yesterday, but couldn't track him down. Shana said it was his day off. He hadn't been at home either."

Purvis covered Chef's body with the sheet and motioned for Luke to follow him. They went down a hall to a large office. Purvis pulled a file off his desk. "That stab wound isn't the only reason I called you down here. We've got at least a two-month backlog for toxicology, but the mayor's office called me and wanted it rushed, so it's been rushed. I should have it in the next day or so, but I found a white substance on Chef's hands and on his clothes. I had your crime scene investigators swab it for me and run it there at the lab. It's cocaine."

Perplexed, Luke questioned, "What was Chef doing with cocaine?"

"I don't know, but it's more than we typically find with someone using."

Luke pinched the bridge of his nose between his eyes. He squinted. "What do you mean? Like he's handling it?"

"Exactly. We will have to wait for the toxicology to see if he was using, but right now, it looks like he was at a minimum handling cocaine."

Luke wasn't exactly sure what this meant. No one they had spoken to had indicated Chef had a drug problem, but that didn't mean he didn't. Luke thanked Purvis and headed to his car. He called Miles Carter to ask him to meet him at the 1922 Club. Miles indicated that he'd meet Luke there in thirty minutes.

Luke navigated his way to the 1922 Club and parked around back. He stood looking at the century old building, pondering the years of illegal activity that had happened there, and was still apparently happening. He checked his watch. Miles was late.

Shana had given Luke the key when she was formally interviewed at the police department the previous day. Luke unlocked the side door to the club and stepped inside. He took a walk through the sitting room and across the hall back into the dining room where Chef's body was found. It looked like a cleaning crew had already come because the floor was clean and the room returned to its normal state, almost as if nothing had happened.

Staring at the spot where Chef's body was found, a chill ran down Luke's back. He didn't like the house at all. Every creak and pop made Luke more on edge. No place had ever done this to him, and he felt a bit silly for feeling this way. He walked through the double doors into the commercial kitchen. It was spotless, but Luke still had no way of knowing what if anything was missing. Just then, he heard a motorcycle in the drive and headed to the side door.

Miles walked into the building as Luke stepped into the sitting room. Luke appraised him while shaking his hand. Miles was taller than Luke by an inch or two, had dark slicked-back hair and a muscular build. He certainly looked like he could handle his own and was bigger than Chef.

"What can I help you with, Detective?" Miles inquired. He stood with his shoulders squared and legs apart, as if bracing for a fight Luke wasn't going to give him.

Luke relaxed his own posturing, hoping Miles would do the same. "I just need to ask you a few questions. Shana said you might be able to help me. Let's head into the kitchen."

Luke let himself be led back into the dining room. Miles seemed to avoid even looking at the spot where Chef was found and Luke took notice.

Once they were in the commercial kitchen, Luke asked, "Is it hard to see the spot where Chef was found?"

Miles looked shaken for a moment. His voice monotone, he mumbled, "Yeah, Chef was a friend. His death was tragic. We are concerned with what happened, especially not knowing who was responsible."

Luke challenged him. "I heard that you didn't get along with Chef?"

Miles took a visible breath before answering. He admitted, "We had our differences, sure. I wasn't happy to be passed over for a promotion, but I understood it. Chef was hard to work for but he ran a good kitchen. We all admired his work ethic and what he'd accomplished."

Luke didn't believe a word he said. "Can you tell me anything that's missing in here?"

Miles looked around the kitchen, opening drawers and cabinets and looking on open shelves. "Not that I can see."

Luke pushed, "What about the knives?"

Miles looked in the drawer. He looked to Luke. "Chef had his own set of knives. I'm not seeing all of them here. He sometimes left with them."

"Specifically, what's missing?" Luke demanded, coming over to stand beside Miles as he went through the drawer.

"His large chef's knife and a small carving knife." Miles eyed

Luke and asked, "Why does this matter?"

Luke snapped, "Everything matters in a homicide. What can you tell me about the drugs, cocaine specifically?"

Miles' eyes roamed around the kitchen. He didn't seem to land on one spot. He definitely didn't make eye contact with Luke. After moments of silence, Miles conceded, "Follow me to the basement."

CHAPTER 9

I spent the morning following up leads that I had dug up the night before. Chef Mouton had a handful of investors for his restaurants in Little Rock. I called each one but none of them seemed to indicate that the restaurants were in trouble. That made sense to me. I had been to them a couple of times, and they were packed, always a long wait even with reservations. I asked if they knew Chef's other investors in New Orleans and Memphis or anything about those deals gone bad. No one seemed to know a thing. A few seemed caught off guard at even the mention of it.

I wasn't getting far. There was no murder weapon found yet. No news coming from the medical examiner or the police. I tried Rhonda one more time. I know Cooper said she had been ruled out, but maybe she could give me something she didn't give them. She didn't answer so I left another message. As I was hanging up, Dan appeared suddenly at the side of my desk.

"What do you have for me?" he demanded. Dan leaned back on my desk with his arms folded over his chest, ankles crossed. He didn't look happy.

"I don't have any more than I had yesterday. I have a couple of quotes about how great Chef was and how much he will be missed, but nothing I know you're wanting."

Dan furrowed his brow. "This won't do. What did your boyfriend say?"

I cocked my head to the side. "You know I can't write what he told me. Besides, he didn't give much away. I'm not saying they don't have any leads, but I don't think they are having any better luck than I'm having."

Dan snarled, "Then tell me why you're here sitting on your ass when you should be out there digging up the dirt?"

I smiled up at him. He's so grouchy. "I'm going. I just needed to run down a few leads, and I wanted to see your handsome face this morning."

He rolled his eyes at me. "You're hilarious," he said sarcastically. "I don't want to see you back here until you've got something substantial."

Then pointing a finger at me, he added for good measure, "If you get scooped on this story, you're fired."

It was my turn to roll my eyes. He'd never fire me. He told me often I was one of the best reporters he's ever had. I didn't really have any leads to follow, but I couldn't just sit and have Dan glare at me. I decided I would head back to Doe's and see if I could pick up any more gossip and go from there. Not that my hips needed another cheeseburger but all for the story.

It was a cold day but the sun was shining so I decided to walk. Doe's was only a few blocks. As I was approaching the entrance, my cellphone rang. It was Rhonda finally calling me back. I stepped to the side, out of the way, and answered. I barely got out "Hello" before she blurted out, "Can you meet me? I really need to talk to someone about Chef."

I turned around and walked briskly back to my car. I drove out of downtown and up into Hillcrest where she wanted to meet. Rhonda said she'd feel comfortable meeting at Abbi's

Teas & Things. It was a tea shop on Kavanaugh in Hillcrest. Kavanagh was a long winding road, connecting Little Rock's most historic neighborhoods, the Heights and Hillcrest. Given how close it was to Luke's house, I knew exactly where Abbi's was located but had never been inside.

Abbi's took up the entire downstairs of a house converted into a business. It had a wide front porch and homey feel inside. It was a bit like walking into someone's living room. Couches flanked the sides of the room and a counter was at the back wall. I liked the place immediately. There were only two women in the place. One I assumed was Abbi behind the counter and the other I figured was Rhonda based on the description I had been provided. She was tall, slim and had shocking white blonde long hair. Her face was probably once pretty, but too much Botox has given her a stiff, unnatural look.

"Rhonda? I'm Riley." I extended my hand. I said hello to Abbi and took in her tea menu. I ordered the cherry chamomile. Once we had our tea, Rhonda motioned for me to follow her farther into the house, and I followed. The place offered several rooms of chairs and tables. We took the one farthest away from anyone. Not that there was anyone else in the place, but if there were, they'd have to seek us out. I could see why she wanted to meet here.

I pulled out my notebook and pen. Some reporters carried iPads and other devices, but I preferred pen and paper. It was less intrusive, and I could maintain eye contact while I jotted down notes.

She looked down at my pad and bit her lip. "I need this off the record for now. You can take notes just don't put my name down."

I agreed and she continued. Her voice was uneven as she

creaked out what she came to tell me. "I knew Chef was in trouble. There was someone blackmailing him. I didn't want to tell the police because I didn't want to cause trouble, but it's been bothering me. What if it's connected to who killed him?"

I couldn't answer that for her because there was a chance it was connected. I encouraged, "Why don't you just tell me what you know, and I can help you sort it out."

Rhonda looked around and leaned across the table to get closer to me. Barely above a whisper, she explained, "He got calls sometimes when we were together. I heard him telling the person he didn't have more money to give them. He said if they were going to go public, to go, that he couldn't pay anymore. Once when I was at his place, there was a rock thrown through his window. When I asked him about it, he wouldn't tell me. He just said someone knew about his past and wanted to expose him."

I jotted down a few notes, trying to make sense of it. "But you don't know the secret?"

Rhonda shook her head no. She wrung her hands. It was easy to see she was distressed by the entire thing. She kept looking out the window and back at me.

"What do you know about his past?" I asked a bit cautiously. She looked ready to bolt.

Rhonda widened her eyes. "Nothing. He never told me. All he ever said was that he had gone through a rough patch several years ago and had straightened out his life. I asked what he meant, but he never explained more."

"When was the last time you saw him?"

Rhonda looked down at her lap. She started to say something but stopped. I ventured a guess. "Did you keep seeing Chef after Marcus found out?"

37

"We did," Rhonda confessed. She started to cry. "I really loved him. I just couldn't seem to stay away from him. I was going to leave my husband, but we never got the chance. When they found Chef dead, I immediately thought it was Marcus. But the cops said his alibi checks out."

I left out my entire encounter with her husband. If I were her, I don't know that I would have risked Marcus' wrath a second time. Frustrated, I asked, "Do you know anything that might help me find who killed him?"

"Just one thing," Rhonda offered. She looked around the room. "Chef always told me if it all went bad, his secrets were buried at the 1922 Club."

CHAPTER 10

Luke took cautious step after step, following Miles down into the basement of the 1922 Club. The stairs were old and dimly lit. It was easy to see why bootleggers had loved the spot. The basement couldn't be accessed from the interior of the home, only from the outside on the back porch. Double doors pulled up from the ground opened the way into the cavernous underbelly of the home.

The basement steps led right into an open room. Miles stepped into the room and tugged on a string hanging low in the middle of the room. An overhead light blinked once, twice and then stayed on, illuminating the room. The dirt floors and cobwebbed ceilings did little to calm Luke's nerves. He clicked off the flashlight he held in one hand while his other patted the gun on his hip. Luke took in the floor to ceiling shelves packed full of stuff including some canned goods that looked like they had been there since the 1950s. Other shelves just held cardboard boxes the contents of which were anyone's guess.

Miles looked around the room and explained. "No one comes down here anymore, except Chef. The club doesn't use this for storage anymore. When Shana started, she went through the boxes and moved important papers and other items to the top of the house where the offices are located. The rest just sits here."

Confused, Luke asked, "What does this have to do with the drugs?"

Miles walked farther into the room. Luke looked behind him back towards the door and then followed Miles. At the far corner of the room, not visible from the entrance, was a shelf filled with holiday decorations. Miles went to one end of it and began to slide it forward. Miles motioned for Luke to look behind the shelf. There was a door that wasn't visible when the shelf was in front of it. It had a padlock on it that didn't look that hard to break. The door itself was made of older wood. Luke assumed it could be easily kicked in.

Miles shrugged. "I've never been in there. I don't have the key, but I think what you're looking for is behind this door."

"I don't get it," Luke said perplexed. "Do you know what's behind the door?"

"Not exactly," Miles offered. "Chef often meets guys down here. I followed him once and saw him going into the room. I suspected awhile ago it was drugs, but never had any real proof."

"You don't have any proof of drugs being sold here?" Luke demanded.

Miles shook his head no and held up his hands. "I swear, man. I knew Chef was up to some shady stuff. I tried at first telling management here, but they didn't want to listen. They just said I was complaining because I didn't get promoted. No one took it seriously."

Luke didn't believe him but didn't have time to argue. He walked back out of the basement and placed two calls. One to Shana to see if she had a key. She didn't but confirmed Chef was the only one with access. She had long since turned the only key over to him because Chef claimed he was keeping some kitchen items down there. She never thought to question him. Luke asked if she was okay with him breaking down the door. She was. Luke called Captain Meadows and explained the situation. He asked for some crime scene techs. Captain Meadows said he'd get right on that. He also let Luke know Cooper was on his way over.

Luke waited for Cooper to arrive and the two of them headed back down into the basement. Luke introduced Cooper to Miles and instructed Miles to stand back. Cooper kept an eye on him while Luke kicked in the door. The first kick rattled the door and the second, harder and with more force, broke the wood and lock.

Luke pulled open what was left of the door. He switched on his flashlight and stepped inside. The light illuminated long tables that held bricks of solidly packed cocaine. There were scales, other packing materials, and several prepaid cellphones. He searched for a light and finally found a switch on the wall next to the door. The room was empty other than the tables. Luke walked out and gave a nod to Cooper, who then motioned for Miles to head out of the basement.

When the three of them were back out in the fresh air, Luke turned to Miles and demanded, "I'm going to ask you again. When did you first become suspicious of Chef selling drugs?"

"What did you find in the room?" Miles countered.

Luke shook his head no. He said more forcefully, "I'm asking the questions. Just tell me what you know or we could get you as an accessory." Luke didn't know how true that was since it was Miles who showed him the room to start with, but Luke wasn't giving an inch.

Miles caved. "I heard him on a call about three months ago. I wasn't sure what he was talking about at first. Then I saw him heading into the basement with a guy once early in the morning before the club opened and again late at night. I started to suspect, but as I said, I never had any real proof."

Cooper had his hands in his pockets and was rocking on the balls of his feet as he listened. He remarked doubtfully, "You wanted Chef's job. You expect us to believe that you suspected Chef of doing something illegal and you aren't going to take the steps to bust him?"

Clearly frustrated, Miles protested, "Listen, you guys got this all wrong. I wasn't that upset about the job. I really did like Chef. He was a ball buster to work for, but he ran a good kitchen. Plus, I didn't really know what was going on. I didn't want to get fired so after I went to management once, and they didn't do anything, I let it slide. I figured no one else cared why should I? I tried to get more information but couldn't."

Luke countered, "When did you find out about that room?"

"Last week. I finally got curious enough that I came down here one night after everyone left and looked around. I found the door behind the shelf but didn't have a key and couldn't get in." Miles stared at them blankly.

Luke wasn't sure what to make of the look or the man. Before they could question him further, crime scene techs showed up. Luke asked Cooper to escort Miles back to the station for further questioning because they hadn't even touched on his alibi or details surrounding Chef's death. Luke needed to process this scene.

CHAPTER 11

I wasn't too sure what to make of my meeting with Rhonda. On my way back, I called Dan to let him know I had connected with her, but that I couldn't use what she said on the record.

"Dammit, Sullivan. Get us something we can use," he snapped and then slammed his office phone down in my ear.

Cellphones took away all the pleasure of slamming a phone down. I was pretty sure that was one of the primary reasons Dan just didn't use his cellphone. Not a lot of satisfaction in clicking "end" on the screen.

As I drove back toward downtown, I thought about the last thing that Rhonda had said. She indicated that Chef had told her all his secrets were buried at the 1922 Club. I felt like if I was going to make any headway, I'd need to head back to the club. I took a drive by the club but noticed Luke's SUV next to a crime scene tech van in the driveway. I couldn't snoop if they were there. I debated for half a second if I should stop anyway, but there was no way they'd let me wander around the scene.

I headed up Cantrell into the Heights. I decided to stop at Starbucks. I could see if there was anything I could dig up about Chef's past on my iPad and wait for Luke and Cooper to leave. I knew coming to Starbucks was a mistake as soon as I walked

43

in the door. Two of Maime's friends were sitting at a table, one with her kid in a stroller. I didn't know their names, but I knew their faces. I had seen them with Maime before and photos of them together on Facebook.

Their eyes were on me as soon as I walked in the door. I headed to the counter to order. I made small talk with the girl who worked there. I was in enough that we knew each other. I picked a table at the opposite end of the store from where Maime's friends were but they were glaring at me. It was hard not to look up to see if they were still looking. I could feel their eyes on me. My name was called, and as I grabbed my coffee off the counter one of them jeered, "I can't believe you actually thought George liked you. You're nothing to look at compared to Maime."

I ignored it. There was nothing wrong with the way I looked, but Maime and I were different. I was taller than she, thick-hipped and long auburn hair. My face was pretty but plain or so I'd been told. Maime was tiny. She was maybe five-foot-two, very thin and shoulder length blonde hair. Her face was always overly made up but her pointed nose and thin lips gave her a pinched appearance. I didn't find a thing attractive about her, but I probably wasn't the best judge.

I sat back down at my table, tried to forget they were there, and started my search for Chef. A few minutes later, the women were standing at my table. They both had the same stick-thin figures as Maime but more attractive. Their hair, one dark, one blonde, shoulder length and straight. Make up and clothes more suited to Rodeo Drive in LA than the Heights, but that's how some of these women rolled. It made me smile. If it made them happy, who cares, but right now I wasn't in the mood to get into it.

I snapped, "What do you want?"

The dark-haired one laughed. "We want you out of our city. You don't belong here."

The blonde one added, "You thought you could steal George away and you can't. Why don't you just head back north with your tail between your legs like the loser you are."

The two of them cackled like they had one over on me.

I took a deep breath and laughed with them. "If Maime wants a cheater by all means, she can have him. I'm not interested. I have more self-respect than that."

Then I got serious. I looked the dark-haired one in the eyes and hissed, "I'm not leaving, and there's not a damn thing you or Maime can do about it. Did you hear I'm dating a cop now?"

They looked at each other and back at me. The blonde snarled, "We'll get you to leave. You can be sure of that."

With that, they turned and left. A few people around Starbucks turned to look at me, but I pretended not to notice. I went back to looking at my screen.

After a few minutes, I tried Luke on his cell. He didn't answer so I tried Cooper. I thought the call was going to voicemail, but he picked up finally. "What's shaken, baby?" Cooper teased.

I laughed out loud. "As my way of playing nice and sharing information, I thought I'd tell you I met with Rhonda."

"You playing nice?" Cooper exclaimed. "Never." He gave another hearty laugh.

"What are you doing? Aren't you working?" I asked, puzzled by his jovial attitude in the middle of the day and wondered if maybe it had to do with his company the previous night.

"Yeah, just brought the sous-chef into the station for questioning. Luke is back at the club. I was just sitting here thinking about not being a cop anymore so you know, I'm happy."

"I see. Well we can get to your mid-life crisis a little later," I bantered. "I want to tell you about Rhonda."

"Go on then, stop keeping me in suspense," Cooper coaxed.

I explained Rhonda's call and meeting with her and then got to the most important parts. "She told me that someone was blackmailing Chef about his past, and that all his secrets are buried at the club."

There was silence on the other end of the phone. "Coop, are you there? Did you hear what I said."

Cooper's tone changed. He was more serious. He said evenly, "Are you sure about this?"

"Positive," I deadpanned. "What's going on?"

"I don't think this is public yet so don't run a story, but Luke found cocaine stashed in the basement of the club. Miles, the sous-chef, told us Chef was selling it. Luke is still at the club with the techs."

I blurted, "Do you think Miles is the one blackmailing him?"

"No idea, but thanks for telling me because it's definitely something I'm going to find out."

CHAPTER 12

I pulled up the driveway of the 1922 Club just as the crime scene techs were leaving. Luke was standing in the driveway. He had a look on his face I rarely see. His eyes were pinched and he was frowning. He looked a bit lost. I parked and walked over to him.

He gave me a half-hearted smile and inquired, "You here as my girlfriend or as a nosy reporter?"

I scrunched up my nose. "Both," I said hesitantly and shrugged. "Cooper said you were still here. He told me about the drugs. I gave him some info about a meeting with Rhonda. I thought I'd head over to see how you were doing."

"You shared information with us?" Luke exclaimed incredulously. Then he pulled me into a hug, something he rarely does in public while on the job, let alone at a crime scene.

I wiggled out of his embrace. "I share sometimes," I balked. "It's not like I don't tell you guys anything."

He kept his hand on my arm. "I know," Luke conceded. "But it's rare. I'm glad you're here though. I need to talk through this case."

He motioned for me to follow him inside. He must be stumped to give me such access. At night at home, he'd shared a few case details here and there, but for the most part, he was

47

fairly close-lipped.

He showed me where Chef had been found. Just like the last time I'd been in the club, I was impressed with the restoration. It definitely maintained the charm I imagined the original home had when it was built. After a quick look at the dining room, Luke and I headed back to the sitting room. We each took a chair.

Luke began, "Tell me what you found out when you spoke to Rhonda."

I crossed my legs and leaned on the sidearm of the chair, getting comfortable. "I think the most important thing she said was she continued on with the affair after her husband found out, and that Chef was being blackmailed."

"Blackmailed?" Luke pondered. He shifted in his seat, resting his forearms on his knees and looked down.

"Yeah, she said someone was blackmailing him about his past. She said she heard him tell someone that he didn't have any more money to pay. She also said he had a rock thrown through his window at home."

Luke got up and started pacing around the small sitting room. He finally stopped and leaned against a bookcase. "I don't get this case. Chef is a fairly noted public figure here in Little Rock, but as I'm sure Cooper told you, it looks like he was selling drugs out of the club. Not just a small amount either. We've got some large quantities down there."

I wondered out loud, "Was he selling drugs to make enough money to pay the person blackmailing him or was someone blackmailing him about selling drugs?"

Luke smiled at me. "That's why I need your logical brain."

"Who are your suspects so far?" I asked.

Luke cocked his head to the side and assured, "Off the record?"

48

I hesitated, "Yeah this part, but will you let me run a story about the drugs?" Before Luke could answer, I pleaded, "My editor is annoyed with me. I need something to run with if I'm going to help you."

Luke conceded, "Run the drug info and that maybe someone was blackmailing him, but nothing else. Try to get a statement from Shana. I want to get her on the record if you can about how much she knew. She's all business with us."

Circling back around I asked, "Suspects?"

Luke counted out three. "I think we've got Miles for sure. I don't trust him. Marcus as well. He may have an alibi, but it doesn't mean he couldn't have used someone to bump off Chef. And even though I'm not thinking it's likely, we have Rhonda. Then there are many unknowns. The drug angle opens the door to any number of people. Deal gone wrong or trouble with his supplier. We just don't know."

"Damn, no wonder you look lost."

Luke smiled and countered, "I don't look lost. I look confused. This case sucks. Too many factors at play. Too many variables."

I stood. "Mind if I take a look around for a bit? Rhonda said something about Chef saying all his secretes were buried at the 1922 Club. He probably meant the drugs in the basement, but I just want to check things out myself."

Luke swept his hand in an open and inviting way, "It's all yours. Just don't touch anything."

I looked around the sitting room, pulling out books from the shelves and putting them back. I wandered into the dining room and back into the commercial kitchen. Nothing seemed out of place. I checked out the back porch and noted that the back of the house was closer to the river than I realized. It was maybe two hundred yards to the river's bank. It seemed to drop off from grass to river rather sharply.

I came back into the house through the kitchen and met back up with Luke in the dining room. I wasn't sure what I was looking for and told him that. He humored me in the way he does sometimes. I ran my hands over the wall, taking in the fine wainscoting. The tables were pristine in their setup, plates, silverware, and glasses all lined up perfectly in order. The fireplace was magnificent. I stood in front of it and turned to Luke.

Catching his eyes, I admitted, "This would have been a lovely house to have lived in. I can picture us having dinner in front of the fireplace and enjoying evenings in the living room."

Luke smiled the way he does when I catch him off guard, which is rare. "You picture us living together? I thought that was a no-go topic."

I shyly admitted, "I think about it often. I don't know that I'm quite ready yet, but soon."

Just when I was at my most vulnerable, my clumsiness got the better of me. I tripped over my own feet. I braced myself against the fireplace. My hand landed square on one of the corner moldings. When it did, a secret compartment in the wall popped open right next to the fireplace. The opening was tucked in behind the mantle so unless you were on top of it, it was hard to see.

Luke saw it, too. Neither of us said a word. He took a few steps and was standing next to me. I looked inside and couldn't believe what I was seeing. Wrapped in cheesecloth was a large bloody knife. I looked up to him bewildered. "I think we found the murder weapon."

CHAPTER 13

After leaving the 1922 Club, Luke took the knife in for processing. He was hoping to get a confirmation that it was the murder weapon, although the recently dried blood on the blade was a good enough indicator that it was. Luke was hoping for prints or other DNA, something that would reveal the killer.

Back and settled at the police station, Luke and Cooper were standing near their desks in the middle of the room on the floor of the police department that held the detective's bureau. Most detectives had gone home for the evening, but Cooper and Luke were giving Miles some time to stew before grilling him again. So far, luckily, the guy hadn't asked for an attorney, but he hadn't given much info either. He also had no alibi or at least one he was willing to give up.

Cooper looked at Luke with a mix of astonishment and amusement. "What exactly were you two doing when Riley stumbled and found the knife?"

Luke sat down at his desk and kicked his long legs up on the chair next to him. He leaned back, running his hand down his stubbled face and laughed. "Nothing, man, just talking."

Cooper toyed with a pen in his hand. He looked back at Luke. "Where's Riley now?"

Luke flipped through a stack of crime scene photos he had on his desk. He was hoping to catch something in them they hadn't seen the first time. Distracted he said, "She went to her office to break the story."

Cooper threw the pen at Luke's head. It fell short of its goal, but it was enough that it made Luke look up and over at him. He furrowed his brow. "What the hell was that for?"

Cooper shot him a look. "I'm your best friend. What's up with you two? Is it getting serious?"

Luke shrugged and deflected. "I could ask you the same thing about your mystery date last night."

Cooper didn't take the bait. Instead, he asked, "Why do you always keep her at bay with these cases? Riley is as good a detective as either one of us. She just doesn't wear the uniform."

Luke shrugged. "She's still a journalist. She could write about something she shouldn't."

"Has she ever betrayed your trust?" Luke didn't answer so Cooper did for him. "She hasn't."

Luke knew Cooper was right. He was also the only person Luke would allow to talk to him that way. Having been friends for nearly twenty years gave Cooper a perspective Luke didn't always agree with but appreciated.

"And another thing," Cooper added, pointing a finger that Luke smacked away. "You need to stop being so by the book. This is why I hate police work sometimes. There's no room for doing things differently. I'm quitting as soon as this case is over. I'm going to be a private investigator, do cases my own way."

Luke chided, "You say that every case but never do it." He looked up at the clock. "Come on, let's go see if Miles is ready to talk."

The two walked down the dimly lit hall to the interrogation

room. The building which housed the police department was old, dating back to the turn of the century. The tile floor was scuffed and looked like it had probably been forty years since it had been cleaned properly. It was just old and worn. The interrogation room was just a table and three chairs. Two on the side near the door and one on the other side of the table. Four walls, no windows, and an annoying fluorescent overhead light that hummed.

Miles looked up as soon as Cooper and Luke walked into the room. They each took a chair across from him. As soon as they sat, Miles looked between the two of them and said defiantly, "I still don't have any more to tell you. I didn't know about the drugs, and I didn't kill Chef."

Luke cautioned, "This will be a lot easier in the long run if you just help us out. See I think you killed Chef, but Cooper here doesn't believe you did it. Either way you know a lot more than you're telling us."

Miles eyed Cooper and asked cautiously, "You don't believe I killed him? Why?"

"I don't think you have the balls to do it," Cooper said matter of fact. "It takes a certain kind of person to take a life, and you don't strike me as someone with that kind of guts."

Miles lurched forward as if wanting to say something. His face was getting red, it flamed up from his neck to his cheeks, but he didn't say anything. After a few seconds, he relented. "You're right. I didn't kill Chef. I'm not saying I didn't think about it from time to time, but he wasn't worth sitting in jail for murder."

"You just blackmailed him," Luke said. He crossed his arms and kicked his legs under the table, crossing them at his ankles. He leaned back in his seat and assessed the scared looking man across the table. Miles licked his lips and rapidly shifted his eyes between Cooper and Luke. He debated for several seconds too long. Luke knew he had him.

CHAPTER 14

Miles didn't say anything for several minutes. The three of them just sat there in silence until Cooper turned to Luke and said excitedly, "That makes total sense. This chicken won't stand up to Chef. Pissed he didn't get the job. Once he found out about the drugs, he used it to his advantage."

Turning back to Miles, Cooper looked right at him. "You might as well get something out of the deal, right?"

Miles just watched him, but still didn't speak. Cooper continued, "You started bleeding him dry financially, but he didn't have anymore. You threatened him, but he's tired of paying. How much did you get him for total?"

Luke leaned across the table and locked eyes with Miles. "You need to tell us or we could easily get you on murder. You had means, motive, opportunity, and no alibi to speak of. You could have easily sneaked up on Chef and stabbed him."

Miles shook his head no, but he was starting to sweat. The room was cold, which gave away the beads of sweat forming at Miles' hairline and beginning to make their way down his forehead. His face was flushed and his breathing, as far as Luke could tell, was uneven.

Luke lobbed the final bomb at him. "We found the murder

weapon. It was hidden in a secret part of the wall near the fireplace at the 1922 Club. Now, how many people do you think know that's there? Not many, only someone with a good deal of access and who knows the history, like an employee."

Miles dropped his head to his hands. Luke and Cooper exchanged a look, but neither said a word. Luke knew they had pushed hard enough. Miles looked up, rubbed his eyes with his hands, and conceded, "I blackmailed Chef, but I didn't kill him. I really don't know who did. You have to believe that."

"Tell me about the blackmail," Luke demanded.

Miles looked a bit relieved to tell his story. He leaned back and breathed out slowly. "Chef didn't know it was me or at least I don't think he did. I had him leave me cash in random spots around the city. I gave him the location to drop it, and I'd wait to pick it up. I sent him emails from a fake account and used a burner phone. I threatened to expose him. I said I found out about the drugs going back three months. It's more like six. I overheard phone calls. I thought about trying to get him fired but figured no one would believe me. I didn't know for sure about the room in the basement until about a month ago and by then I was already blackmailing him."

Cooper asked again, "How much did you get him for in total?"

"About fifty grand," Miles admitted. "I tried to go higher, but Chef said he didn't have it. It didn't seem like he was stalling or not wanting to pay. I believed he didn't have it. I didn't want him to go to the police."

"If he's dealing all those drugs, where's his money going?" Luke asked, a bit confused by what he was hearing.

Miles shook his head, "I don't know. It didn't make sense to me, but I believed him. I also heard him arguing about money a couple of times on the phone. He was in debt to someone."

Luke believed him. "Did you hear the rumors about bad business dealings in the past?"

Miles nodded yes. "I think everyone's heard those rumors but his restaurants here are a success. It sounds like he had restaurants that failed in other cities awhile go. Do you think that's connected to this?"

Luke didn't confirm or deny, but he wondered exactly how many people Chef owed money to and if it was enough to get him killed.

After getting a formal statement in writing, Luke called in some officers to take Miles down to the city jail for processing. Luke wasn't sure if Miles had killed Chef or not, but if he did, he wasn't giving it up easily. He'd stew in city lockup until a bail hearing. If Miles turned out not to be good for the murder, Luke didn't think he would get much jail time for blackmail with a dead witness and cash drops, but maybe even a little jail time would at least serve some justice.

Luke and Cooper headed for their desks to grab their things and head home for the evening. On their way out of the building, Luke asked, "Did you get much from those investors? I forgot to ask."

Cooper shook his head no. "They didn't tell me a thing. If Chef was in debt to any of them, they aren't giving it up. I put a request in to pull Chef's financials. Maybe something in there will give us something more."

Before getting into his SUV, Luke turned to Cooper and asked, "You think if I call Riley and give her the scoop on Miles' arrest for blackmail, she'll be happy?"

Cooper smiled and slapped Luke on the back. "She'll probably want to marry you."

CHAPTER 15

After finding the murder weapon, I raced back to the newsroom. I tried calling Dan on the way, but he wasn't answering his cell or his desk phone. I knew most of the reporters had probably gone home or were on late assignments out of the office. That's how the newsroom always was at dusk. When I got to the street in front of the building, I was happy to see Dan's office light on. I entered the building while I continued to obsessively stalk my phone, checking the Little Rock Times, the other local newspaper, as well as the three main news stations' websites to see if anyone was breaking the news about the drugs. I didn't think anyone would be, but you never knew in this town, given how fast gossip spreads. No one had the story so far. If I hurried, I'd make the eleven o'clock news with my scoop.

I raced up the steps and hit the landing where our offices were located. It was set up much the same way the police department was with desks in the center and offices lining the perimeter. I didn't warrant an office, just a desk. It wasn't even a cubicle, just an open desk in the middle of the room, flanked by other reporters' desks.

I quickly made my way to Dan's office across the room in the very front of the building. As I scooted by my desk, I threw my bag. It hit dead center and bounced to the floor. I ran up to Dan's door and bumped it, shoving it open harder than I meant. He looked up at me, his eyes wide and mouth open. His door banged off the wall and sprung back in my face. I stopped it with my hand and steadied it. I was out of breath, disheveled and excited.

"I got a scoop!" I yelled, trying to get out each word and catch my breath at the same time. "Not only did I find the murder weapon, but Chef was selling drugs out of the basement of the 1922 Club."

"Is that it?" Dan teased, barely containing his smile. "The way you charged in here, I would have thought you'd caught the governor with his pants down on Main Street."

I shot him a sideways glance and slumped down into the chair across from his desk. I caught my breath for what felt like the first time since stumbling and finding the knife. Dan looked at me expectantly, and I laid out the whole story detail by detail. Finishing, I boasted quite proud of myself, "I've got the scoop, too. No one else is running it, and Luke said he'd keep it quiet until I broke it."

Dan took a sip of water from a glass on his desk. His eyes peered over the rim at me. I felt like he was judging me for something. I don't know what I could have possibly done wrong. I got him his story. "What?" I snipped.

He shook his head and put his glass down. He stared at me for a few seconds. "How are you going to spin finding the knife? I told you to get me the story not become the story."

I opened my mouth to speak but didn't have a good retort. I just stared back at him, hoping something witty would pop into my brain. It didn't, but before I did more mental gymnastics, he burst out laughing, a good hearty belly laugh that I don't think

I've ever heard before. I looked at him like he was losing his mind.

Through snorts of laughter, he said, "I'm teasing you. This is just the funniest thing I've heard in a long time. You literally tripped over your own feet and found the murder weapon. The cops searched the house top to bottom. They let you into the crime scene and you find it just because you're clumsy."

I'd be offended but he wasn't wrong. Luke wasn't happy his team hadn't found it first, but even he admitted it was by chance we found it at all. Nobody was looking for secret storage spots in the wall.

Dan stopped laughing. He dismissed me in the way he does best. "What are you still doing here? Go write the damn story! You've got the cover of the paper tomorrow and the homepage above the scroll. Give me your best fifteen-hundred words."

As I headed back to my desk, I remembered that I promised Luke I'd call Shana before I put the story out. Luke had wondered if I'd get further with her than he would. He really wanted the element of surprise to see if Shana would panic if she knew a reporter was going to break the news about findings drugs in the basement.

She answered quickly like she was sitting on top of the phone. When I told her, she was genuinely shocked and promised she'd call Luke to find out what she needed to do and how the management of the 1922 Club could be of assistance to resolve it all. She gave no indication that she knew or wanted to hide it like most people do when they want to bury the truth.

Before I hung up, I asked her about secret hiding spots in the club. She informed me that there were many. The original house had been built that way, but she wasn't sure that outside of staff and management if members of the club or visitors knew of them or where they could be found. I told her about finding the potential murder weapon and let her know Luke would be in touch about that once he confirmed. When I secured two solid quotes from her, I got down to writing.

The story wrote itself. My fingers were busy, hitting key after key on my laptop when my phone rang. It broke my concentration, and I grumbled to myself as I searched in my bag for my phone. It was Luke. I answered only to tell him I'd be done soon when he detailed Miles' arrest for blackmail. I cheered for him so loudly, Dan yelled for me shut up and keep writing. I looked in his direction, flipped him off, and thanked Luke for being the best cop and boyfriend a girl could ask for.

Less than ninety minutes later, I was sending Dan my final for him to edit and proof before publication. I stood while he read over the copy. His face broke into a rare wide grin. "You did good, kid. Real good."

CHAPTER 16

I had just pulled into my driveway and put the car in park when my cellphone rang. My Bluetooth picked it up, and I looked at my dash display but there was no number. It was listed as a private call. I hesitated answering, but I thought better of it and clicked to answer. Before I could say anything, a muffled voice on the other end of the line barked, "You're looking in the wrong place."

"What?" I asked, confused by what they meant. "Who is this?" I could barely make out what they were saying. I also couldn't tell if it was a man or a woman. I turned up the volume, hoping to hear better.

"You are looking in the wrong place," they said again, more insistent this time. Then they explained slowly, "Chef didn't defraud investors in Little Rock. He's in deep with a guy out of Chicago. Gambling debts. A failed restaurant. He owes hundreds of thousands. He's got Chef running drugs to pay the debt back."

"Who is this? How do you know this?"

"Consider me a friend. Look into it. Roman Marcello. You'll find your killer." Then the call ended with a click.

I scrambled to find my notebook and pen to jot down the name before I forgot it. Once I wrote it down, I sat staring at the phone, waiting for them to call back. After a minute when I realized they wouldn't, I called Luke. He answered quickly and was happy to hear from me, thinking it was just a quick chat. His voice grew serious as I explained my call. He said he'd be over in about forty minutes.

I went inside and made sure the door was locked. The hairs on the back of my neck were standing up. I didn't like that the caller had my cellphone number. I wasn't hiding it, but it wasn't public either. I tossed my bag and coat on the living room chair and went straight back into the kitchen. I dug around in the fridge until I found some sliced deli turkey and cheese. I pulled the rye bread from the counter and made a sandwich. I stood at the kitchen counter and was just about to take a bite when there was a knock on my front door. I checked the clock on the wall behind my stove. Luke should be here soon, but he had a key.

I put my sandwich down, wiped my hands on a dishtowel, and went to the front door. Thinking it was probably Luke or even Emma, I unlocked and opened the door without looking. That was my first mistake. The second was letting in my visitor. It was my ex, George Brewer. His dark hair was in need of a cut but other than that he looked the same. He was about five-foot-ten and had a stocky build. I'd say he had a handsome face, but I hated him so he was ugly as hell to me. Most women didn't share my opinion. To anyone else's eyes, he was classically handsome. He was also very married.

I stood in the doorway, hand on my hip. "You shouldn't be here," I snapped.

He looked at me sheepishly and asked, "Can I come in? We need to talk."

I debated for a moment but didn't want Emma to see him. I

foolishly stepped out of the way to let him in, but only backed up a few feet. George wasn't getting beyond the living room. He reached to grab a strand of my hair, and I knocked his hand away, stepping back out of his arm's reach. I shook my head no. Both hands on my hips now, I said matter of fact, "You wanted to talk. You have five minutes."

"Can we sit?" he asked, looking into my living room at the couch.

"No. Talk or leave."

George ran a hand down his stubbled face. He looked me up and down. "You look great, you know that right?" he asked with a sly grin. "I wish we didn't have to deal with all this. I really do wish things had turned out better."

I threw my hands in the air. "This is what you came here to talk about?" I asked completely frustrated. "We don't need to rehash the past." I grabbed his arm and forcefully turned him around, shoving him back to the door. I wasn't doing this again. I was over it emotionally, but it didn't mean I kept wanting to dig into an old wound.

"Stop, listen, okay," he said resigned, worming out of my grasp. "I'll tell you what I really came for. Maime is pissed. She's on a rampage. I just came to warn you. She and her friends want you out of Little Rock, and I'm worried at what lengths they will go to make that happen."

I asked incredulously, "And you think by coming here, you're helping that?"

He didn't say anything, just looked down at his feet. He knew he was wrong, knew he was just stirring up trouble. For some reason, he didn't want me, but couldn't stay away. Frustrated and tired, I implored, "Just go back home, convince her she's all you want and leave me alone. Once you do that, she will leave me alone."

I walked to the door and opened it. "Please leave and don't come back."

He stood his ground. "I'm not leaving, Riley. We can find a solution that works for both of us. I'm not giving up on us."

I tipped my head back and laughed. This was getting old. "There is no us, George," I hissed. "There wasn't then either. You were lying to me. I found out, and it was over. I've moved on. You are married. Leave me alone."

George took a step towards me, but not to leave. His hands were outstretched as if he were going to embrace me. Before he could, I felt a presence outside, angry and ominous.

CHAPTER 17

I turned to look out the door as I heard Luke's voice low and even the way it was when he was angry, close to completely losing his temper, which was rare.

"She asked you to leave twice now," Luke growled. He opened the screen door wide and stepped in front of me, shielding me from view with his body.

George and Luke squared off. I tried to step around Luke to get in between them, but Luke prevented me with his arm. He was stronger than I realized sometimes.

Luke, his voice serious and on the brink of losing his temper, snarled, "You have no business being here. Riley has asked you to leave. Now go and don't come back."

I was waiting for a punch to be thrown. Luke knew about George. He knew from start to finish how the whole sordid relationship went down. He didn't know George was still trying to contact me, and Maime and her friends were harassing me. Luke was protective, and it would have sent him into the rampage I was worried was about to erupt.

The energy hung dense and thick between them. It was a standoff in every sense. It went on for several moments. Thankfully, George finally stepped around Luke and left without saying another word. He didn't even look at me. I hoped it would be the last I'd see of him.

I shut and locked the door. When I turned, Luke wrapped his arms around me. I could feel the tension leave his body. I knew he wasn't angry with me. Kissing me on the forehead, he asked softly, "You okay?"

I pulled back and looked up at him. "I'm fine," I said seriously and meant it. "He just keeps stirring up trouble."

"Is there more I should know?" Luke asked, eyeing me, searching my face for the truth.

"No. Don't worry. I'm fine," I lied. He had more on his plate than he needed. He certainly didn't need my past relationship drama right now. "Let's go eat something and talk about that phone call I had."

We went into the kitchen. I pulled out some leftover chicken soup and heated it for both of us and fixed Luke a sandwich. I didn't have much to offer him but at least had that. As I was getting the last of it together, Luke opened my fridge to get us something to drink. He looked inside and then turned to look at me and laughed. "You really need to go to the grocery store. You're down to stale mustard. When we live together, I'm going to take much better care of you than you do yourself."

I can't lie, a bit of anxiety started to bubble up. I breathed deep. Not that I didn't want to live with Luke. Falling in love with anyone and being that serious after everything that happened with George shook my confidence a bit. If I were being completely honest with myself, it scared the hell out of me. He looked so sweet and eager to move us forward, I didn't have it in me to tell him I was scared of being with him like that.

"Yeah, it's been a couple of weeks since I went. I've been living on take-out," I admitted. "I'll go this week." I carried the plates over to the table.

Luke took a bite of his turkey on rye and spooned his hot chicken soup. "Tell me about this call."

I took a sip of tea and explained, "Roman Marcello. Does that name mean anything to you?"

Luke shook his head no. "Should it?"

"The caller said that Chef had gotten in deep with a guy in Chicago for hundreds of thousands of dollars. Some gambling debts and a failed restaurant. Chef was running drugs as a way to pay off his debts. The caller gave me the name Roman Marcello."

Luke weighed the information. He asked thoughtfully, "Any indication on the caller? Man or woman? Anything particular about the voice you remember?"

I thought for a moment, but there wasn't. "It was muffled. It was either a deeper sounding woman or a man with a more feminine voice. It was really hard to tell. They didn't seem to have a particular accent or say anything that would hint about the region of the country they are from."

Luke kept watching me. Frustrated, I laid my hand on his arm. "Sorry, it was so muffled that it was hard to hear them at all."

"It's okay," Luke said with disappointment in his voice. "Just keep your phone close in case they call back. In the meantime, I'll give Cooper a call, and we can start to run down some leads there."

Luke picked up our dishes and put them in the sink, running water over them. To his back, I asked, "Did you confirm the murder weapon or get any more from Miles after you called me?"

"Lab still has the knife. Probably won't know anything until morning," Luke said, turning and leaning against the counter.

He paused, chewing on his bottom lip, and then said, "Miles is a different story. We got some truth, but I don't think we got it all."

"What do you think you're missing? Do you think he killed Chef?"

"I don't know. He could have. Miles knows the club as well as anyone. Chef was balking on paying him more hush money. Chef got the job he wanted. Miles knew Chef's schedule, he could have easily got into a confrontation and stabbed him. When Chef fell to the ground, Miles really took out his rage."

"But?" I coaxed.

"But it doesn't feel right. I don't think he did it, except I don't have anything logical that tells me he didn't."

"Trust your gut," I encouraged, picking up the last of our dinner on the table and carrying it to the sink. "If you don't think he did it, he probably didn't."

"I'm out of suspects then, unless the lead in Chicago pays off," Luke said, stifling a yawn. He reached over and tugged a strand of my hair. "I'm going to shower."

Luke rarely stayed at my place. We were mostly at his in Hillcrest. His bed was bigger and he had to be at work before I did. It was just easier, but I guess he was staying the night. I finished the dishes and put them away. I hated going to bed with a messy kitchen.

I walked through the house, making sure doors were locked and shutting off lights. By the time I made it upstairs and into my bedroom, Luke was passed out asleep. He looked so peaceful. I covered him with the blanket and chastised myself for feeling any anxiety about moving forward in my relationship with him. I got myself ready for bed and crawled in next to him feeling grateful.

CHAPTER 18

Luke was out of bed before the sun came up. He made the drive to Hillcrest to shower and grab fresh clothes for the day and beat Cooper to the station. Luke was about thirty minutes into an exhaustive internet search and a search of the federal and state criminal databases looking for anything he could on Roman Marcello. He turned up quite a bit including old drug, racketeering, and even an assault charge. Luke was about to call a detective in Chicago when Cooper arrived. Luke started to fill Cooper in on Marcello when Captain Meadows yelled for both of them to come into his office.

They each took a seat at his desk. Flipping through some papers in front of him, Captain Meadows asked, "What's the status of the investigation?"

Cooper looked to Luke, letting him take the lead. Luke explained, "We are coming along. You have my initial notes there on the blackmail and drugs and the arrest of Miles Carter. As you know, we found the murder weapon—"

"Exactly how did that happen?" Captain Meadows interrupted. "Why was a reporter allowed access to our crime scene?"

"Well…" Luke started but wasn't sure what to say. He didn't have a good explanation.

"Yeah, yeah." Captain Meadows waved his hand at Luke

dismissively. "Just tell me you weren't having sex at the crime scene."

Cooper stifled a laugh.

Luke swallowed hard. "Captain," he reassured. "It was nothing of the sort."

Captain Meadows shook his head in disgust. He reprimanded, pointing a finger between the both of them. "No reporters at our crime scenes. I don't care if she's Sherlock Holmes reincarnated. Got it?"

They both shook their heads yes, duly chastised. Luke said, "I'm running down another lead about a guy in Chicago Chef might have been connected to. We got a tip he owed him money. That's maybe where the drug angle comes in. Other than that, Miles Carter is still in lockup for blackmailing Chef."

"What are you sitting here for?" Captain Meadows growled. "Go run the Chicago lead to ground. I need something to give the mayor."

Cooper and Luke were dismissed. Once back at their desks, they split up tasks. Nearly an hour later, Cooper turned to Luke and said, "Marcello might be our guy. That burner phone Chef had, has calls in and out to Marcello."

That got Luke's attention. With a prepaid phone, they weren't going to have any luck getting real records for calls. Surprised, Luke asked, "You confirmed Marcello's number?"

"Simple enough," Cooper explained. "I just blocked our number and called all the numbers in the call log. Got his voicemail."

"All right," Luke said. "That confirms the connection. Now, where is he?" Luke had Marcello's full rap sheet. The last time he'd been in prison was four years ago. He did two years for assault.

Luke placed a call to the Chicago Police Department. After being routed through a series of people and being put on hold for longer than Luke had patience for, he was finally connected to a Detective Michael Agostino. Agostino filled Luke in on all sorts of interesting facts about Marcello. He wasn't firmly connected to the Chicago mob, but he wasn't unconnected either. He had family ties, but his level of direct involvement was still up for debate.

Agostino informed Luke that Marcello had been running drugs in the city for years. He had quite a big operation, some detectives speculated it went across state lines, but nothing had been proven. Agostino also confirmed that Marcello had run gambling operations but also had legal investments like bars and restaurants. That wasn't the most interesting fact. It was what Agostino said next that floored Luke.

"It's interesting you're calling," Agostino said. "We traced Marcello to Little Rock a few days ago. What's he done this time?"

Luke took a second to recover. "We think he was supplying a large amount of cocaine for sale here and possibly murdered one of his dealers."

"Wouldn't put it past him. Let us know how we can help," Agostino offered.

"Any idea where he's staying in the city?" Luke asked hopefully.

It sounded like Agostino set the phone down and was shuffling papers. The commotion stopped, and he was back on the line, detailing, "Yeah, there's a downtown Marriott we traced his credit card to. That's how we knew he was in Little Rock. We were trying to bring him in for questioning for another assault here so we ran his credit after days of surveillance turned up nothing."

"Thanks, we are going to bring him in for questioning. I'll be in touch," Luke assured him.

Luke gave Cooper the short of it and they both headed out. Luke called for backup to meet at the hotel. He told the officers to stay outside and out of sight, hoping he wouldn't need them. Luke also called the hotel to confirm what room Marcello was staying in. The clerk at the desk told Luke Marcello just got back and was definitely in his room. Luke said they'd be there in ten minutes and to delay him if he started to leave.

CHAPTER 19

Two hours later and without incident, Luke was sitting across from Roman Marcello in one of the police station's interrogation rooms. Cooper and Luke had gone to Marcello's hotel room, knocked and when the man answered, they explained they needed him for questioning. He came willingly, but that didn't mean he was giving anything up that easily.

Luke had gone around and around and Marcello wasn't giving an inch. Cooper had tried, too, but he didn't make a dent. Marcello explained he knew Chef, that yes, he had invested in his Chicago restaurant that went belly up, but he didn't know anything about drugs or even that Chef was dead.

Marcello ran a hand through his slicked back, black hair and challenged Luke, "If I killed him, why would I be sticking around? I'd get the hell out of the city before you'd even know I was here."

"Tell us about the drugs," Luke demanded, changing tactics. "We know that you were supplying him. He was selling cocaine to pay off the debts he owed you. We already had a witness give us a statement."

Marcello didn't flinch. He slumped down farther in his chair and tapped his finger on the table. "Who's this witness?" Then he said confidently, "They got nothing on me."

Luke was about to press him when the door opened and Cooper interrupted, "Luke, I need you for a second." Luke got up leaving Marcello to stew.

"What's up" Luke asked as the door closed behind him.

Cooper handed him a report. "We got the details back on the knife. It had Chef's blood on it. Pulling a print was harder, there's a mess of Chef's blood on the handle. The only print they could pull is unknown."

Luke looked over the report. They didn't get a DNA match on the killer, and given the unknown print, they couldn't definitively pin it on Miles or Marcello with the murder weapon anyway. Both of their prints were in the system. Didn't mean they didn't wear gloves either.

Luke tucked the file under his arm. "You got anything else? Anything I can use?"

"Actually, I do," Cooper said, his face cracking a wide grin. "We pulled Marcello's prints from one of the scales that were in the basement and on the lock. He's definitely been down there with Chef."

"I can work with that," Luke said, finally feeling like he was catching a break.

"I don't want to put a damper on that, but how's he looking for the murder?" Cooper asked.

Luke shook his head. "I don't know. Don't have a sense of that yet."

Cooper crossed his arms and leaned against the wall. "The only thing that's bugging me about this guy is how'd he know where to hide the knife?"

"Unless Chef pointed out hiding spots inside the club, I don't know," Luke said resolved. "But I'm going to find out."

Luke went back in armed with the additional information. He slapped the report down on the table. Luke knew it didn't contain anything useful to the murder, but Marcello didn't know that. Up until he slapped the file on the table, Marcello looked bored and ready to bolt. Looking at the file, he sat up straighter in his chair.

Before Marcello lawyered up, Luke got right into it. "Your prints match those found at the scene of Chef's murder. We've got an eyewitness who saw you. You're going down for this murder so I'd start talking. We've got enough to make an arrest right now."

Marcello was out of his chair in a flash. He shouted across the table at Luke, "I never went anywhere near that dining room. I've only ever been in the basement of the club. I didn't kill him!"

Luke was standing at that point, too, squared off on the other side of the table from Marcello. Luke realized Marcello's mistake a few seconds before the other man did.

Marcello started to say something and then stopped. He tried again and stopped. He finally gave up and admitted, "You're right about the drugs. But it was the other guy that killed him. I saw him standing over Chef."

"What guy?" Luke demanded.

"He's tall, dark hair. I think he worked with Chef. I don't know his name. I'd recognize the face."

Luke darted out of the room, leaving Marcello just standing there. Luke grabbed a photo of Miles off his desk and brought it back in. He slapped it down on the table in front of Marcello. "This the guy?"

Marcello picked it up and seemed to study it carefully. "Yeah, that's him."

76

"Sit," Luke commanded, pointing at the chair. "Tell me what you know."

Over the next hour, Marcello confirmed what Riley had heard. Chef had some gambling debts and a failed restaurant. Marcello had convinced him to sell the cocaine locally to make the money back. Chef didn't want to, Marcello said, but he didn't give the man much of a way out otherwise. The morning Chef died, Marcello was there in the basement with Chef, dropping off a supply and picking up some cash. Chef got a call on his cell and needed to go upstairs. Chef told Marcello to stay in the basement out of sight. Marcello said Chef never came back so he finally left the basement, locking the door behind him and putting the shelf back in front of the door. Then he went in search of Chef.

The back door was locked, he said, so he went around to the side. That was locked, too. Marcello said he noticed a motorcycle in the driveway and walked around the building looking in windows. That's when he saw who he now knows as Miles standing over Chef's body. He saw Miles pick up the knife with some kind of cloth and walk across the room. Marcello said he couldn't see what Miles did with the knife, but he hightailed it out of there before he was seen. He'd only stuck around in Little Rock to connect with another drug supplier. He had merchandise to move.

He closed by saying sarcastically, "It's not like I can fly the cocaine back to Chicago, and I wasn't going to drive twelve hours across a few states with that much cocaine in the car."

Luke believed him. He left the room, had uniformed cops come in and make a formal arrest on Marcello for the drugs. Luke went to city lockup to attempt one more time to get a confession from Miles.

CHAPTER 20

I spent the day working on a few different stories. There were a couple of arraignments and sentencing hearings that day. I wrote a few short articles that covered the newspaper's online crime section. Nothing earth-shattering, but the day flew by. Now it was dark. The rain had started to pound on the streets in front of the building, lightning flashed off in the distance, and I had even heard we were under a tornado watch. I debated whether or not I should hold off walking to my car. The newsroom had mostly emptied out already. Dan's light, of course, was still on. I don't think he ever went home.

I made my way to his office and nudged open the door. Dan's head was down, going through some articles. "Hey, boss," I said as I entered, "it's really coming down hard out there. You staying awhile?"

"Until it lets up," he said still looking at the papers in front of him.

I cleared my throat loudly. Finally, Dan looked up with a blank look on his face. "Do you want something?"

"Luke called. They are pressing charges on Miles Carter for Chef's murder. They didn't get a confession, but looks like it's a pretty solid case," I explained from the doorway. "I sent a copy to the digital department so it will go online tonight. I'll be at the arraignment in the morning."

"Good, good. Looks like that wrapped up fast," Dan mumbled, still distracted.

I turned to leave, but stopped and called over my shoulder. "You need a date," I said teasingly.

"I'll write your dating profile when you're ready."

He growled at me and then laughed. "Don't get swept up in the tornado, Dorothy," he yelled to me as I started down the steps.

About fifteen minutes later, I was in my car and heading out of the city. Even though I had carried an umbrella, I was fairly drenched from the rain and wind that was coming down sideways.

As I came around the bend on LaHarpe, connecting to Cantrell, I noticed what looked like light from a flashlight bouncing around inside the first floor of the 1922 Club. Luke had told me earlier they had asked staff not to go there. They were going to search the place again. My wipers were working hard to keep up with the pounding rain, but I could still see the light inside the club.

It defied all logic, common sense and safety, but I turned into the driveway to check it out.

Lightning flashed and the roar of thunder quickly followed. The storm was right on top of me. I pulled into the back of the club and noticed a black SUV. It looked like a Lexus, but I couldn't make out the model. I texted Luke that I thought someone was sneaking around the club, and he should probably send an officer over to check it out.

I waited for nearly fifteen minutes. No one came out of the club, and the cops didn't show. I noticed the light though.

There was definitely someone in the place. I fished for the wet umbrella that I had thrown on the backseat floor. The cold rain pelted me as soon as I put a foot down on the wet pavement. I ran to the backdoor but it was locked. I stood on the back porch while lightning flashed and thunder boomed again. I took a big deep breath and sprinted to the club's side door. I was surprised when the handle turned and the door opened.

I took a step into the sitting room, moving out of the rain. "Hello," I called out. "Shana? The cops are on their way."

I heard distinct movement in the dining room, a shuffling of chairs. I saw a flashlight beam hit the hardwood of the dining room floor across the hallway. "Hello?" I called out again.

I took a few tentative steps, crossed the hall and poked my head into the dining room and nearly got my head knocked off from a shadowy figure swinging a large brass candleholder in my direction. I stumbled a few steps and turned just in time to duck out of the way as they swung it again. I knocked over a chair, and the table I leaned on for support wobbled. I got myself upright and looked to see who was trying to bash my skull in.

CHAPTER 21

Rhonda was standing there, disheveled and wet, with the candleholder high above her head. She looked poised to take another run at me.

"Stop!" I yelled. "Rhonda, it's Riley from the newspaper."

"Riley?" she asked. I confirmed. She brought the candleholder to her side. "You shouldn't be here," she said matter-of-factly.

Cautiously, I took a couple of steps back, feeling uneasy. "Rhonda, what are you doing here? How'd you get in?"

Rhonda looked out the window and back at me. She seemed to be debating what to do. "I'm looking for my earring. Chef brought me here a few times. I lost it the last time I was here. I need to find it."

With skepticism in my voice, I said, "The cops will be here soon."

"Riley, you really shouldn't have called the cops," Rhonda said, shaking her head. She was agitated. She said with anger in her voice, "I need to find that earring. I can't let anyone know I was here."

"They are going to know," I said, hoping to hear the cops pull into the drive at any second.

"They can't know!" she screeched. "They have the killer in

jail. They can't know I was here. It will all fall apart."

I wasn't sure, but I thought she had started to cry. She wasn't making sense. I said calmly, "I don't know what you're talking about. Who can't know you were here?"

"The cops!" she yelled again. "Why are you so nosy and stupid? I called you. Told you where to find the killer. You found him. You don't need to be here. This is none of your business."

"That was you that called me? Why didn't you just tell me that when I saw you?"

"You ask too many questions," she mumbled. Almost as if talking to herself, she said quietly, "I'm going to have to kill you, too. I don't want to kill you, but they can't know. They can't know. But someone knows. They hid the knife. Someone saw me."

Looking at me with eyes wide, she asked, "Do you know who hid the knife?"

I took a step back towards the sitting-room door. Rhonda wasn't stable. That much was clear.

She followed me with her eyes. When she realized I was heading for the door, she struck at me again. I dodged her, and she crashed into the wall.

"You killed Chef?" I asked, trying to make quick sense of what she was saying. "I thought you loved him."

"I did love him," she said, "but he was ruining everything, just like you."

I tried to get to the sitting room doorway but she was blocking it. She didn't budge and didn't say a word, just watched me, the candleholder still firm in her grasp.

"I can help you find your earring," I coaxed. "Just tell me what happened and it can be our secret. The cops already made an arrest. They are charging Miles in the morning. Just tell me what happened while we look for your earring. I'm sure whatever happened was Chef's fault."

She debated for several moments. I thought I nearly had her, but she charged at me, swinging the candleholder. She caught me on the shoulder, and I yelped out in pain. I grabbed for her arms, and we struggled to the ground. We were hitting and kicking at each other. I finally knocked the candleholder from her hands and it went sliding across the floor. She took a swing at me. I dodged it and caught her chin with my fist. Her head snapped back and then forward. I wasn't wasting any time, I punched her again. She collapsed back on the ground while I stayed ready to hit her again.

Just then heavy boots pounded into the sitting room. During the commotion, I hadn't heard a car. The overhead light flicked on and I blinked, shielding my eyes from the bright light.

"What the hell is going on?" Luke shouted when he saw us in a tangled heap on the ground. He took in Rhonda's bloody face. Then he looked at me. "Are you all right?"

Luke, Cooper and some other officers were standing around us. I'm sure they were trying to figure out what had happened. Neither Cooper nor Luke looked happy to see me in the middle of their crime scene. Hopefully, what I found out would soften their annoyance with me.

"I'm fine," I exhaled. "Help me up and arrest her. She admitted to killing Chef. I didn't get details, but she said she did it."

CHAPTER 22

It was close to eleven when I finally made it to Luke's house. Cooper drove my car while Luke finished processing Rhonda. Luke didn't want me to drive or go home alone. He was worried about my hand. It was bruised and a bit swollen from connecting with Rhonda's face, but it was nothing too serious. I could have driven myself and gone back to my place, but Luke wasn't hearing it.

When I arrived at Luke's, I took a long hot shower. Then I made some hot tea while Cooper started a fire. I handed him a cup and snuggled into my favorite chaise chair and wrapped myself in a blanket. Even with the hot shower and roaring fire, I still felt a chill.

Cooper looked at me thoughtfully. I felt like I was about to get a lecture, but he surprised me. "We should do this more often," he said with an air of determination.

I looked at him sideways. "We should do what more often, relax in Luke's living room or have me fighting with your suspects?"

He laughed but got serious again. "You're wasting your talents writing for the newspaper. Don't get me wrong, you're a great writer, but you're an even better investigator."

"That's crazy," I said, but actually didn't think he was too far off the mark. "Even if I was, I don't want to be a cop."

Cooper sat on the couch, leaning forward with his arms resting on his knees, eyes on me. He said excitedly, "That's the beauty of it. You don't have to be a cop. I'm quitting the force. I already decided. I'm getting my private investigator's license and going into business for myself. You should join me."

"You're really doing it?" I asked in disbelief.

"I'm really doing it," Cooper said determinedly. "I haven't told Luke yet and won't until it's a done deal. I've got a bit in savings and taking the state test next week. If I pass, I'm giving my notice. You in?"

"Good for you." I meant it. "I'll think about it, but can't make any promises. I think you'd be great at it though."

Before Cooper could respond, we both turned to the front door as Luke stepped into the room. He looked tired but had an air of relief about him.

"That was really stupid," he scolded and then added softer, "but I'm glad you're okay."

"Sorry," I said sheepishly. "I knew no one was supposed to be there. I had a feeling. Did she confess?"

Luke grabbed a glass of water from the kitchen and then took a seat on the couch with Cooper and filled us in. Rhonda had confessed. She said Chef had broken off the affair, but she couldn't accept it. She kept calling and showing up at his house and at work. Rhonda eventually found out about the drugs because she found the basement doors open on one of her unannounced visits. She couldn't find Chef anyplace else so she sneaked down.

She saw Chef talking to Marcello. She saw the drugs with her own two eyes, which forced Chef to explain. She had lied to me when I interviewed her. She knew his secrets all along.

She was calling me to throw me off track.

Rhonda told Luke that Chef wasn't giving in. He said he was done so she went to the 1922 Club that morning to confront him. They got into a huge fight that started in the kitchen and ended in the dining room. Rhonda had grabbed the knife along the way. Chef never thought she'd use it, Rhonda had explained. He kept telling her to put it down, but he didn't try to grab it from her or hurt her. Chef wasn't the kind of man to strike a woman, and that's really what got him killed. Even after she stabbed him, he didn't fight back. She thought he was in shock.

They both were, but Rhonda said she was also full of rage. She doesn't remember stabbing him more in the back after he fell. She just remembers all the blood, dropping the knife, and running from the room. Rhonda said she burned her bloody clothes in the firepit behind her house, but knew she had lost an earring. That's why she called to pin it on Marcello. She needed to throw off the cops. She hoped they wouldn't find out.

Luke also added, "Miles showed up that morning to the 1922 Club not long after Chef was murdered. He saw Chef's body and the knife and hid it in the wall. Miles assumed people would think it was him that killed Chef, and he knew his prints were on the knife from having used it in the kitchen. He tried to wipe off the knife with the cheesecloth but there was too much blood. He figured it was better the cops never solved the case than pin it on him."

"The call that interrupted Chef and Marcello and brought him upstairs was from Rhonda," Luke continued to explain. "But she had gone by the time Miles showed up. Marcello just assumed it was Miles that killed Chef. Had Rhonda not come back for the earring, we'd probably never know."

I said with satisfaction, "See, if I hadn't meddled, the case wouldn't have been solved. You'd have charged the wrong person."

Cooper and Luke both laughed at me, shaking their heads, knowing that all the grouching at me in the world wasn't going to stop me sometimes. I think Luke secretly appreciated my help. Cooper left for the night, and Luke and I got ready for bed.

"Another one solved," Luke beamed as he snuggled into bed. "I haven't been sleeping well, but think I will tonight." He pulled the covers back for me to climb in next to him. He put his arm around me and nuzzled my neck.

"We should talk more about moving in together," Luke said sleepily before he started to softly snore.

I murmured okay. I don't even know if he heard me. I knew he was waiting for a definitive answer from me and a plan. I felt pressured, but it wasn't Luke's fault. I knew we had to progress, and I wanted to. I was just scared. I didn't know if I could live up to Luke's expectations.

Right before falling asleep, I thought maybe I'd just go back to New York and save Luke the inevitable heartbreak of finding out I wasn't really who he wanted. I guess time would tell what would happen.

About the Author

Stacy M. Jones was born and raised in Troy, New York, and currently lives in Little Rock, Arkansas. She is a full-time writer. Stacy holds masters' degrees in journalism and in forensic psychology. Stacy is an avid reader of the mystery genre. Whether a reader likes their mysteries more hard-boiled or prefers a cozy, Stacy offers two series – the more hard-boiled Riley Sullivan Mystery Series and the cozy Harper & Hattie Magical Mystery Series.

You can connect with me on:
- http://www.stacymjones.com
- https://twitter.com/SMJonesWriter
- https://www.facebook.com/StacyMJonesWriter
- https://www.bookbub.com/profile/stacy-m-jones
- https://www.goodreads.com/StacyMJonesWriter

Subscribe to my newsletter:

✉ http://www.stacymjones.com

Also by Stacy M. Jones

Follow Riley's Next Steps - Read Deadly Sins
   Now available on Amazon.

Join Stacy's Mystery Reader's Club for all the behind the scenes on her new releases, exclusive deals and content & to access her free Starter Library. Subscribe at http://www.stacymjones.com/

If you like your mysteries a little more cozy, don't forget to check out Stacy's Harper & Hattie Magical Mystery Series. There is a **free novella Harper's Folly** available through the Starter Library.

Please leave a review for The 1922 Club Murder. Reviews are a great way for Stacy to grow her readership & allow other readers to find her books more easily.
Amazon: amazon.com/author/stacymjones
   Facebook: StacyMJonesWriter
   Goodreads: StacyMJonesWriter

Deadly Sins

A suspect in a serial homicide. A hard-headed detective out for revenge. The private eye who stands between them. Private investigator Riley Sullivan is a woman on a mission to find the missing wife of a man she once loved and prove he's not responsible for the murdered women found floating in the river. Det. Lucas Morgan is the lead homicide detective intent on stopping her.

Can the two put their past aside to find the missing woman and stop a serial killer terrorizing an upscale suburb? Riley must battle her own emotional demons to untangle a web of lies, find a killer, and keep herself from becoming the final victim.

Made in United States
North Haven, CT
31 March 2022

17721129R00061